A Max & Colby Adventure

ZOOMING FUN

Janis Hennessey

Illustrated by Teresa Street

ISBN: 13 978 1493773541
ISBN: 10 1493773542

To my husband Barry,
our children Evan, Meg, and Jared
who loved Max and Colby.

How can Max, a beagle, who loves to zoom all over the yard and Colby, a hound mix, who loves to sit and watch the clouds be best friends?

1. Friendship - Fiction, 2. Animals - Dogs, Ages: 2 - 8

BigTree Press
55 Applevale Drive
Dover, NH 03820

Table of Contents

Where to buy more Max & Colby backyard adventures:

Amazon.com

ZOOOOOOOM!

Max *raced* across the backyard.

He *hurried* around the swing set.

He *darted* into...

the dog house.

ZOOOOOOOOOOM!

He *ran* out of the doghouse.

He *dashed* behind the sandbox.

He *whirled* close to...

the big tree.

"What are you doing, Max?" asked Colby as Max ran twice around the big tree where Colby was resting.

"I am...

zooming!"

"*Zooming* is running fun," barked Max.

He *flew* between the wheelbarrow and the flower garden and...

jumped through the sprinkler.

Then, Max stopped right next to...

Colby.

"What is running fun?" asked Colby.

Running fun is *racing* all around just because...

I am happy," said Max getting ready to *zoom* again.

"What do you like to do when you are happy?" asked Max *darting* around the bikes.

Colby said, "When I am happy I like to...

watch the clouds."

"Sit and watch the clouds with me, Max," said Colby.

But, Max was already *zipping* around...

the soccer balls.

"I do not want to sit and watch the clouds," said Max.

"Colby, come *zoom* with me!" called Max

as he *rushed* past Colby and into...

the garden shed.

But, Max did not come out of the garden shed.

Colby waited...

and... waited...

and... waited.

Finally, Colby walked over to the shed and...

ZOOOOOOOOOM!

Max *shot out* of the shed, *ran* past Colby, *zoomed* around the swing set, the dog house,

the sandbox, the big tree, the wheelbarrow,
the flower garden, and...

jumped three times through the sprinkler.

Colby watched Max *zigzag* all around the yard.

Colby thought, "Max is much more fun to watch than...

the clouds."

"Max, we are so different. How can we be friends?" asked Colby.

"We are friends because we like to do many things together," said Max. And, it's okay that we like to do...

different things apart."

"Now I am tired," said Max, getting a drink of water.

So, Colby and Max walked over to...

the big tree.

They watched the clouds for a while.

Then they lay down in the cool grass and took a nice long nap...

together.

Draw a picture of Max zooming around things in the yard.

Draw a picture of Colby enjoying the clouds. Can you make hidden pictures in the clouds, like the clouds on page 29 & 30?

Acknowledgments

I would like to thank each of the wonderful members of my family and friends who assisted me in writing this story. I so appreciated their excellent suggestions and their constant support.

Family: My husband, Barry Hennessey, our three children and their spouses, Evan & Jenn Hennessey, Meg & Chris Scull, Jared & Liz Hennessey, my sister, Karen Dieruf.

Teachers: Mary Chamberlain, Jennifer Connelly, Lauren Schultz, Ann Marie Staples.

Children's librarians: Debra Cheney, Laura Horan, Linda Smart, Susan Williams.
Thank you for field testing the story with various ages of young school children. Your feedback was so valuable and encouraging.

Special thanks to my son Jared who merged the pictures and showed me how to create BigTree Press, and to Linda Pedersen for all the help she gave me in getting my first book up and running.

About the Author

Janis Hennessey, along with her husband and three children, have hosted many pets, including dogs, cats, birds, fish, gerbils, rabbits and even snakes, in their New Hampshire home.

At the age of 10 she began writing neighborhood plays for her friends in Louisville, KY. Over the years these stories evolved into various children's books. She loves to use the real stories of the children and their family pets in her stories.

Janis earned a master's degree in French Literature from University of KY and a diplôme in French History from the Sorbonne, Université de Paris. She has taught French in KY, MA, and NH where she always encouraged her students to write creatively in another language.

The End

Where to buy more Max & Colby backyard adventures:

Amazon.com

Made in the USA
Charleston, SC
27 September 2014